Little Legends: The Big One!
published in 2021 by
Hardie Grant Children's Publishing
Wurundjeri Country
Ground Floor, Building 1, 658 Church Street
Richmond, Victoria 3121, Australia
www.hardiegrantchildrenspublishing.com

Text copyright © 2021 Nicole Hayes and Adrian Beck
Illustration copyright © 2021 Leo Trinidad
Series design copyright © 2021 Hardie Grant Children's Publishing
Series design by Kristy Lund-White

®™ The AFL logo and competing team logos, emblems and names used are all
trademarks of and used under licence from the owner, the Australian Football
League, by whom all © copyright and other rights of reproduction are reserved.

A catalogue record for this
book is available from the
National Library of Australia

Hardie Grant acknowledges the Traditional Owners of the country on which we
work, the Wurundjeri people of the Kulin nation and the Gadigal people of the
Eora nation, and recognises their continuing connection to the land, waters and
culture. We pay our respects to their Elders past, present and emerging.

Printed in Australia by Griffin Press, part of Ovato,
an Accredited ISO AS/NZS 14001 Environmental
Management System printer.

13 5 7 9 10 8 6 4 2

The paper this book is printed on is certified against the Forest
Stewardship Council® Standards. Griffin Press holds FSC®
chain of custody certification SGSHK-COC-005088. FSC®
promotes environmentally responsible, socially beneficial and
economically viable management of the world's forests.

Hardie Grant
CHILDREN'S PUBLISHING

Little LEGENDS

AFL

THE BIG ONE!

ART BY **LEO TRINIDAD**

NICOLE HAYES & ADRIAN BECK

As far as Oz was concerned, Grand Final week was **BETTER THAN CHRISTMAS!**

This time every year, he'd go to bed tingling with excitement from the top of his head to the tips of his toes and dream of raising a **PREMIERSHIP**

CUP to millions of adoring fans; then every morning he'd spring out of bed, itching to get to school to soak in the atmosphere in the build-up to the **big weekend**. Fresca Bay Primary would be plastered with balloons, streamers, home-made banners and more! **Footy** would be the only thing anyone talked about. And Oz would wear his footy scarf the whole time – no matter what the weather was like.

But this year, it wasn't the AFL Grand Final that captured Oz's attention (although that *was* **EQUALLY** as good as Christmas).

No – it was the Coastal League's **GRAND FINAL WEEK!**

The Fresca Bay Falcons were in the Preliminary Finals – and right now, they were just **ONE KICK AWAY** from becoming Grand Finalists!

Oz **streamed** through the centre of the Fresca Bay Oval with the footy, thoughts of **Premiership glory** **WHOOSHING** through his mind. The Falcons were three points down, with only minutes left. But three opposition players from the Longbourne Leopards were sprinting towards him.

Oz knew he had to snap out of his

daydream about the **BIG ONE**, or a daydream is all it would ever be!

He slowed down and looked for options. Ellie had dropped back towards the goal square and was calling for the footy, but the opposition were **RIGHT ON OZ** now. He couldn't get a kick away.

This was **NOT** going to plan.

'Oz!' Sanjay's voice broke through from somewhere behind.

There was no time – Oz had one shot only.

Holding his breath, he handballed blindly over his head. The ball went **HIGH**, **looping** through the air. As Oz spun around to watch, the Leopards ran for the footy. Sanjay had just seconds to get there first.

'Eyes on the ball, Sanj!' cried Oz, shocked that Sanjay seemed to be *leaning forward.*

But no! Sanjay wasn't just leaning forward – he was doing a **SOMERSAULT!** Some kind of Sanjay-style dance move. Then he flicked his legs up into the air and, with the soles of his muddy footy boots, Sanjay **CONNECTED WITH THE BALL!**

The footy flew right over Oz, right

over the Leopards, and high into the air.

'Yesssss!' cried Oz. 'All yours, Sis!'

Ellie dropped back behind her opponent to grab a **chest mark**, but was too far out from the goals. She played on, drawing the Leopard player who was tagging 'Rocket' Rana. At the last second, Ellie handpassed over to Rana, who wasted no time **BOOTING** the footy long. So long that it landed in the goal square, and bounced forward ...

BOUNCE ...
BOUNCE ...
Then up it went!

'Come on!' Oz urged the ball, helpless

to do anything but watch.

The ball took another bounce, then dribbled agonisingly slowly through the muddy goal square ... and finally, *finally*, bounced over the line!

GOAL!

'Woohoo!' cried Oz. He jumped on top of Sanjay, half-wrestling, half-hugging him in the mud. 'Sanj, you're a legend!'

Sanjay **LAUGHED** as they sprang up again to watch the umpire signal a goal. 'All we need now is for the siren –'

Hooooooooooooooooooooooonk!

Rana and Ellie hugged and danced in the goal square.

'GUYS!' Oz cried to his team mates. 'We're in the **GRAND FINAL! YEE HAR!**' he yelled, jumping onto Sanjay.

Splash!

They were both rolling around in the mud. Then came Ginger, Sim, Koa, Paolo, Freddo and the whole Falcons team! It was another **STACKS ON** in the middle of Fresca Bay Oval! The crowd roared. Everything was a blur!

Somehow in the pile, Ellie found Oz and Sanjay, and the three of them leapt up to celebrate in a **HUGE** three-way chest bump, yelling at the top of their lungs,

'We're in the **GRAND FINAAAAAAL!**'

CHAPTER 2

Later that evening, Ellie took out her Hawks notepad from her neatly arranged drawer and placed it on her neatly arranged desk next to her neatly stacked schoolbooks. Then, with her favourite Hawks pen, she wrote '3' in the **GOALS** column under the heading: 'Preliminary Final'.

Ellie had kept track of her goals all year. With a very quick calculation in her head, she discovered she was averaging 4.3 goals a game. **Not bad!** Better than last year – and even better than Jeremy Cameron! Soon she'd done precisely twelve different calculations, measuring how, when, and where she'd kicked all her goals. She loved the way the numbers sat in her head. Especially when they reflected such a **GREAT SEASON**. The Falcons had really given it everything this year. There was just one more challenge left. And it was a big one.

The BIG ONE.

She returned her notebook to its place in her drawer, and took out her Mad Maths Squad folder. The Grand Final wasn't the only thing on Ellie's mind – the Mad Maths Championship was this week too.

Mad Maths was **SUPER FUN!** Not better than footy, of course, just a different kind of fun.

And, Ellie had to admit, it was a little nerve wracking too. She really hoped they would win the Championship this year. Last year she'd **missed out** on the contest because Oz had made her feel guilty about skipping footy training for maths practice – and then the maths team had won without her! She didn't know why she let Oz get to her – but she was determined it wouldn't happen again this year.

Ellie opened the Maths Squad folder and studied the details of the day.

'Whatcha looking at?' Sanjay said, appearing in Ellie's bedroom doorway.

Ellie **JUMPED** in her seat, sending her Maths Squad folder FLYING. 'Thanks Sanj! Ever learn to knock?'

'Sorry! Your dad let me in. And, um, your door was open, so ...'

Ellie sighed. 'Fair enough. Sorry. I got a fright.'

'It's cool.' Sanjay ducked down to pick up the folder and gather the bits that had fallen out. 'Hey – the Mad Maths contest thingy? Isn't it **this week?** I think Principal Wiley said something about it at assembly. It was hard to concentrate with Oz talking the whole time.'

'It's *impossible* to concentrate when Oz is talking. Which is pretty much **ALL THE TIME**.'

They both laughed. Oz did have a habit of talking a **LOT**. Especially when he was meant to be quiet!

Ellie took the folder from her cousin.

'Yeah, the Regional Championship is this Thursday after school. Not that Oz seems to care. I'm not surprised he talked over the announcement.'

Sanjay laughed. 'Nah. Oz will be there. You two do everything together! Like my dad says, you're *joined at the hip*.'

'No, we're not ... just because we're twins doesn't mean we're the same. We're two **COMPLETELY** different people!' Ellie frowned. 'Oz doesn't even *like* maths,' she added, getting more wound up the more she thought about it. 'But it's one of my **favourite things!**'

'Like dancing is mine.' Sanjay dipped his

head and rolled his arms outwards in a perfect wave as proof.

'**Exactly.** At least you understand, even if no-one else does.'

'But I thought Oz was in your Mad Maths team too?'

Ellie snorted. 'Last year – for about **FIVE MINUTES**. And only because his best mate, Jack, was part of the team.'

Sanjay stopped dancing. '**Best mate?** But aren't I ...' Sanjay blushed, then looked puzzled. 'I mean, I haven't met any Jacks in our year?'

Ellie sighed. 'Jack Pang. We used to call him JUMPIN' JACK. He changed schools at the start of the year when they moved house. He used to be a Falcon too, but had to **switch teams**. Must have been before you moved from India.' Ellie returned the maths folder to the desk drawer.

'Oh. Right. Yeah, I have heard of him.' Sanjay seemed to think about that as he shuffled from Ellie's desk to her cupboard. He seemed almost **NERVOUS** to Ellie – bopping around like he didn't want to stand still. **'The *traitor*, right?'**

'That's what Oz called him. Jack plays for the Colburton Cockroaches now – he's their **STAR RUCK**. That's part of the problem.'

'Wait. That's the team –'

'Who slaughtered us a few weeks ago?' Ellie **grimaced** at the memory. 'That's the one. But Jack was overseas then. Hopefully we won't have to play them in the Granny – we'll know after the other Prelim ends.' She looked at her watch. 'Which should be soon.' Her heart **skipped** a little at the thought.

Sanjay's whole face lit up. 'I can't wait to run out for my first Grand Final!'

Ellie grinned at her cousin. **'Maybe you'll kick the winning goal!'**

'Woah. Can you *imagine*?'

Ellie got a bit caught up in that image too, and soon they were both grinning wildly. Ellie grabbed her Hawks footy from the bedside table, and shot a **BULLSEYE-PERFECT HANDPASS** to her cousin.

Quick as lightning, Sanjay caught the ball on his chest. All those years of dancing had **fine-tuned** his reflexes. Ellie was amazed at how fast he could move.

Ellie leapt off the bed, determined to **shake off** her annoyance with Oz. The memories of Jack, and last year's disappointment around the maths contest, were just that: *memories*. This year would be different. She'd make sure of it.

'**KICK-TO-KICK** out front, Sanj?'

'You're on!'

Just as they were about to rush out the door, Oz appeared in the doorway, his face caught between shock and awe.

'What's up, bro?' Ellie said.

Oz held up their dad's phone, pointing to it accusingly. 'The second Preliminary is over. We know our opponents in the Granny.'

Ellie reached for the phone, but all she could see was a pic of Oz pulling a face. Oz was always changing their dad's screensaver.

Oz YANKED the phone back, unlocked the screen and held it up, this time with the Preliminary Final score-line etched across the page.

Ellie's heart **dropped**. 'Oh no.'

'Oh. Yes,' Oz said, his face grim.

Sanjay looked back and forth between them.

'WE'RE PLAYING THE COCKROACHES!' Ellie and Oz yelled together.

CHAPTER

3

Sanjay was getting used to sausages.
It helped not to think **too much** about
what went into them.

Just as well, too, because Aussies
seemed to take any opportunity to whack
'snags' on a barbie and hand them out in
bits of soggy white bread slathered in

tomato sauce. Fortunately, with Uncle Luke in charge of the food, this evening's barbecue promised to be better than the usual **SAUSAGE SIZZLE**. The smell made Sanjay's mouth water.

Both families were gathered in Ellie and Oz's backyard. Prishna, Lenny and Sanjay's sisters, Aahna, Bela and Charu, were playing **chasey** on the grass, with their dog, Scruff-muffin, doing his best to join in. Mostly, that involved him weaving between the girls' feet, threatening to trip them up and almost getting stepped on.

The sun was fading, but the evenings were getting warmer. Sanjay couldn't wait to see some summer action on the beach. **WOOHOO!**

Ellie was up on the balcony, a set of maths books stacked beside her on the chaise. Sanjay couldn't see Oz anywhere. He climbed the stairs, following the balcony as it wrapped around the house, and leant over the balcony to see if his cousin was under the deck. **NOPE.**

'Your dad's got *no* chance against your sisters,' Ellie said, peering over her textbooks at the **CHAOS** below.

Lenny looked up at the deck. 'I heard that, Ellie Little. You ask your dad how quick I was back when we played for the

Falcons. **Fastest in the league**.'

All eyes turned to Luke at the barbie, who grinned. 'Like **lightning**, Len,' he said. 'Especially at dinnertime. Speaking of which, grub's up!'

Lenny's eyes lit up, and suddenly he was like lightning, **LEAPING** to the front of the queue before anyone else had a chance to move.

Luke grinned sheepishly. 'My mistake, mate. A few more minutes yet.'

Lenny's face fell, and everyone laughed.

'You *are* like lightning, Dad!' Aahna said, **GIGGLING** as she tagged Lenny and sprinted away.

Ellie and Sanjay chuckled. His family was a bit crazy, but he had to admit, they were **never** boring.

Still. Something was missing. Or some*one*, anyway.

'Els, where's Oz?'

Ellie sighed. 'How should I know?'

Sanjay blushed. 'Um, I just thought –'

'Because we're twins, we **always** have to be together?'

Sanjay blinked. 'Er, no? It's just that everyone else is down there, and you're the only one up here.' He smiled weakly. 'You've got a better view.'

It was Ellie's turn to blush. 'Oh. Right.'

'Is everything okay?' Sanjay asked.

'Ellie! You need to see this!' Oz's voice came from inside the house.

Ellie threw up her hands. 'See what I mean? I'm trying to **concentrate** on maths practice for Mad Maths, and he keeps interrupting, even though Oz *knows* this is **SUPER IMPORTANT** to me.'

'Oh. Right. That must be annoying?'

'It IS.'

'Well ... good luck with your practice,' Sanjay said. 'You'll **slay** at the contest!'

Ellie blushed. 'Thanks Sanj. Sorry for being grumpy.'

'It's cool. I get it,' Sanjay said, before heading inside in the direction of Oz's voice.

Sanjay blinked at the gloom after coming in from the bright sunlight. The living room blinds were down, and Oz was cast in the TV screen's grey glow.

'Whatcha doing in here? The family's having a **party** outside!' Sanjay glanced over his shoulder, wishing he was out playing chasey instead.

Oz's mouth was a **FIRM LINE** and he was frowning at the TV.

'Huh?' Oz barely looked up.

On the TV was a home video of what looked like the end of a **Falcons game**. Oz and Ellie looked younger – Ellie was the same size as Oz, which was amazing, considering Oz barely made it to her shoulder now.

On the screen, the younger Oz was laughing with a tall, skinny, black-haired boy. They were **joking** and **shoving** each other, mucking around after a game that they'd obviously won. Ellie and Rana were there too – all four of them **HAMMING IT UP** for the shaky camera. Luke's voice came through the video, telling the kids to smile and say hi to Sanjay and the family.

It was **WEIRD** seeing them all together like that without Sanjay. Back when he was still in India, before they were all living near each other like they were now.

'Who's that tall kid?' Sanjay finally asked.

'Jumpin' Jack Pang!' Ellie exclaimed, appearing in the doorway.

'DON'T SAY THAT NAME!' Oz yelled.

Ellie stuck her hands on her hips, frowning. 'I can say it if I want to! He was my friend too, remember?'

Oz **glared** at his sister. 'I thought you were too busy doing stupid maths?'

'I was. But I've finished now. No thanks to you!' Ellie stood taller suddenly. 'And it's **NOT** stupid!'

Oz just grunted.

Sanjay shifted uncomfortably. 'Why are you watching all these videos?' *Especially since it's clearly making you mad,* he wanted to say, but didn't.

Oz rewound the footage and hit play again, squinting at the game play. He slowed the picture down and then sped it up, back and forth, **over and over**. Examining it like a scientist studying a bug through a microscope.

'Homework,' he said gruffly.

'Ha!' Ellie snorted. 'Like you ever do homework!'

Oz glared at his sister. 'Just because you can't get your head out of your books! Who does maths on a *Saturday night*?'

Ellie's face turned pink. 'I have a **PRETTY GOOD** reason, you know.'

'There's never a good reason to do maths!' Oz smirked.

'Yeah. You've made it **PRETTY CLEAR** you think Mad Maths is pointless!'

But Oz didn't seem to be listening. He turned the volume up and flicked through different scenes, fast forwarding the clip, then stopping it on ...

JUMPIN' JACK PANG.

'Are you studying the Cockroaches?'

Ellie peered closer at the screen. 'Or Jack?'

'Both.'

'Jack's still away. He probably won't be playing,' Ellie said. But Sanjay could hear uncertainty in Ellie's voice.

'It's **THE BIG ONE**,' Oz said, like that explained everything. 'You have to be ready for anything.'

Apparently, 'anything' meant Jumpin' Jack Pang. Sanjay stared at the boy on the TV screen. So **THIS** was Oz's former **BFF**. Sanjay had to admit, he seemed like a good player. **REALLY** good. No wonder Oz and Jack were besties.

The flutter in Sanjay's ribs was back,

and it did **NOT** feel good.

'You have to check out my **GRAND FINAL VICTORY DANCE!'** Sanjay said, a little desperately. He stepped into the middle of the room, sliding gracefully through his routine, adding a soft shoe shuffle at the top, finishing with an elaborate bow at the end.

'That's cool!' Ellie said, but to Sanjay, she sounded a little flat. He could tell she was trying to make an effort. It was Oz he was worried about.

But Oz had barely looked away from the TV.

'Seriously, Oz. You missed Sanjay's

whole thing!' Ellie said, frowning.

Oz finally looked at Ellie, and then Sanjay, blinking as though he'd forgotten they were there. 'I'm kinda **BUSY** right now.'

Ellie scoffed and headed back outside.

The flutter had moved to Sanjay's tummy. He thought about what Ellie had said about Jumpin' Jack – how he and Oz must have had all these stories, and history. Years of **playing footy** together, hanging out at school. Sanjay and Oz had only shared emails and letters and photos before this year. They had a **LOT** of catching up to do.

Sanjay shuffled closer to his cousin. 'Oz ... Now that I'm, y'know, here in Australia, well ... we're **proper friends**, right?' Sanjay said.

Oz looked at Sanjay like he hadn't heard right. 'Proper friends?'

'Yeah. You and me. We're good friends, aren't we? Maybe even **BESTIES?**'

''Course,' said Oz, but with a twitch of his head like he thought Sanjay might be going loopy. 'Why?'

'No ... nothing.' Sanjay smiled like it was no big deal, but his heart was **racing**. 'It's just ... er ... ' He shrugged, a little lost. 'It's kinda cool ... and stuff.'

Oz gave Sanjay another funny look. Sanjay's cheeks were **BURNING** now. He stood there for a long second, his mouth flapping, making everything a thousand times more awkward.

Oz blinked, then nodded towards the back door. **'Race you to the snags!'**

Relief washed over Sanjay as he chased after his cousin, the conversation apparently forgotten.

CHAPTER

3

Oz spent Sunday morning creating a huge chalk mural on the back wall of his house. Beneath the deck, he'd drawn the **PERFECT** footy scene. At least, perfect to him. Everyone from school was in the crowd watching as he scaled an impossible number of players to take a

SPECCY at the very top of the pack, Charlie Cameron style. He'd written **'OZZY RULES'** above his heroic face, and **'FRESCA BAY!'** at the bottom of the mural.

'Woah!' said Ellie as she burst through the door, Sanjay close on her heels. 'You look like a human rainbow!'

Oz glanced down at his PJs. Purple, green and yellow chalky stripes crossed his chest.

Sanjay **LAUGHED**. 'Purple looks really good on you, Oz.'

Oz shrugged and turned back to his mural, smudging the outlines of his arms to make his muscles **EVEN BIGGER**.

He might make himself a bit taller too while he was there.

Ellie and Sanjay hung over the deck to inspect Oz's handy work.

'Cool pic!' Ellie said.

'That's awesome!' Sanjay added.

Oz nodded. 'Not bad, hey – **AH CHOO!**' A thick cloud of chalk dust shot up Oz's nose, making him explode in a series of the **BIGGEST**, **LOUDEST**, **SNOTTIEST** sneezes he'd ever managed. If he wasn't so focused on making his mural **PERFECT**, Oz might have been quite proud.

When he finally stopped sneezing, Ellie

was frowning at Oz's artwork. 'Hmm.
Why am I **UNDER** your speccy? When,
you know, I take the speccys in this family.'

'What's the problem?' Oz shrugged.
'We do everything together! We're a team.'

'Not *everything*!' said Ellie. 'Besides, it'd be more accurate if you drew *me* booting **ANOTHER GOAL**.'

Oz looked at the mural – he was really proud of it just as it was. And if Ellie wasn't careful, she was definitely getting a **FART CLOUD** drawn on her.

'Well, at least you're in it, Ellie,' Sanjay muttered.

'Sanj, you're ... um ... ' Oz trailed off as he pointed to a section of the mural where Sanjay clearly wasn't. 'Look, it's not finished yet!'

Ellie rolled her eyes. Oz had **NO IDEA** what was wrong with Ellie, and he could see that Sanjay didn't look happy about the mural either.

Oz sneezed again. His drool was purple. He wiped his mouth, while he studied the picture. Maybe by the goals was a good spot for Sanjay? And over there, on the wing, he could squeeze in Ellie – **cheering Oz on**.

He shrugged again and decided to fix it later. No big deal.

'Did you two want something?'

Before anyone could answer, his dad came out onto the balcony, waving his mobile phone in the air. **'Hey team – big news!'**

Oz thought about what that might be, and one image stuck in his brain.

'Did that video of me trying to wear all my underpants at once **go viral?**' he blurted.

'What? **EW!**' Ellie grimaced.

His dad laughed, then stopped. 'Wait. You did what ... ?'

'Nothing. Forget I said anything,' said Oz. Although, he was pretty proud of his underpants effort, and was sure he'd gotten close to a **record** of some kind—

'Hello? Earth to Oscar?' Ellie was staring at him, while Sanjay was still not looking at him at all. **Weird.**

Luke cleared his throat. 'Anyway, as I was saying – it looks like the Pangs have come back early from their trip.'

Oz blinked. 'The Pangs? **Jumpin' Jack's** family?' His voice was hollow as he climbed the steps to join the others.

His dad hadn't said it out loud, but Oz knew, deep in his belly, what it meant.

'That's great!' Ellie said. But her smile was tight. Oz realised that she knew what it meant too.

There was **NO WAY** the Cockroaches were going to leave out a player as good as Jack Pang from the **Grand Final team**, even if he'd only played a handful of games all year.

Which meant, not only were the Falcons playing the Cockroaches – who'd flogged them by their biggest losing margin this season – but their star player and Oz's ex-best friend, Jack **THE TRAITOR**, would be playing too.

IT WAS AN ACTUAL NIGHTMARE.

'The Pangs want me to cater for their homecoming party.' Luke waved the phone again. 'It'll be great to catch up with them, won't it, kids?'

'Yeah, Dad. ***GREAT***,' Ellie said, but Oz could feel her watching him.

'I know you guys didn't get to hang out

much this year,' Luke said. 'With all their moving and travelling. But now they're back for good. We can visit them in Colburton whenever you want.'

Oz **clutched** the deck railing for support.

Even Sanjay looked worried.

Luke headed back inside, muttering to himself about menu options.

Ellie seemed to be waiting for Oz to say something. But the words **stuck in his throat**.

Finally, Sanjay broke the quiet. 'Well, I'm kinda hoping that we won't even notice Jumpin' Jack –'

'Don't. Say. His. Name!' Oz said, way too loud. Rage rose in him like a wave. 'He's a traitor! The **WORST** kind of person. He didn't just leave our team – **HE JOINED THE ENEMY!'**

Oz was shouting now. Even *he* knew he sounded a bit crazy.

But this was **THE GRAND FINAL! THE BIG ONE!** How dare **THE TRAITOR** show up out of the blue to ruin his life? **AGAIN!**

Ellie could barely look at him, while Sanjay stood there squirming.

'Let's forget about it for now,' Sanjay finally said. 'Do you ... wanna go to the beach?' he added, his voice quivering. '**Bombs off the pontoon** will fix everything. Plus, I still wanna teach you my **VICTORY DANCE**.'

Oz was too wound up. He shook his head. 'You guys go.' He didn't glance back as his sister and cousin left him alone.

Instead, Oz stared at the mural, zeroing in on the image of him taking a speccy on Ellie's shoulders. He knew **EXACTLY** who he'd replace her with now. The one person he wanted to beat more than any other.

The traitorous, *treacherous*, **JUMPIN' JACK PANG!**

CHAPTER
4

Ellie got up well before her alarm on Monday morning, desperate to kick off **Grand Final Week**. Two of her favourite things were happening in the same week! No matter what happened, Ellie was determined to have fun – that's what mattered most.

She hurried out to the kitchen, wanting to be **FIRST** to the favourite new cereal bowl – it had a falcon painted on the side, and was huge, so you could fill it really high. Their dad had found it in an op shop, but he almost didn't buy it because there was only one.

Oz **NEVER** got out of bed even a minute before he had to, so it was the perfect chance to—

'**OZ LITTLE!**' Ellie gasped.

Oz was up to his elbows in his breakfast, an **ENORMOUS** pile of cereal spilling over the rim of the falcon bowl.

As annoying as he was, Oz looked too

much like a greedy chipmunk for Ellie to be super mad. And Ellie knew that as long as Oz was eating, he wasn't distracted by **ANYTHING**. Not even Jumpin' Jack.

'I need lots of energy. Gotta focus on **THE BIG ONE!**' said Oz, who seemed to be channelling yesterday's anger into cereal consumption. If it meant he was out of his grump, Ellie was fine with it.

'Right,' said Ellie, 'and speaking of the Big One, let's grab Sanj and check out what's happening in town before school! Manny's Milkbar will be decorated for sure, and the Bowls Club were going to paint a **Falcons logo** on their lawn!'

'Nice,' said Oz. 'And I think the fish-and-chip shop is offering a **FRIED FALCON BURGER**.'

'Ewww,' said Ellie. 'They might wanna rethink that.'

Just then, **Scruff-muffin** came bounding into the room, his wet tongue lolling. Oz put his hand out to give Scruff a pat, but the dog saw Oz's toy **Geelong Cat** and grabbed it in his jaw, running off down the hallway.

Oz hurried after the dog. 'Back in a sec, Sis!'

After three bowls of cereal, Oz was finally dressed and ready. They met Sanjay out the front, just as Ellie noticed a letter stuck in their letterbox. As the boys wandered ahead, **handpassing** a footy between them, Ellie yanked out the letter. It was addressed to her, and had a Mad Maths logo on the corner of the envelope.

Why were they sending her a **letter?** All the arrangements had been made through school so far.

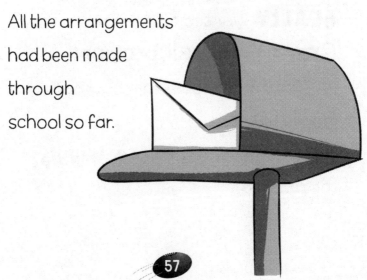

Ellie hesitated. What if she'd been dropped from the team? What if they didn't need her anymore? Or what if the Championship had been **CANCELLED!**

She was almost too scared to look.

'Come on, slowcoach!' Oz called out.

Ellie almost told them to go ahead without her so she could check, but Sanjay and Oz were so pumped, and she **REALLY** wanted to see Fresca Bay's **Grand Final celebrations**, so she stuffed the envelope in her backpack and jogged to catch up.

Sanjay seemed **extra wiggly** as they walked.

'Pumped about the weekend, Sanj?' Ellie asked.

'Huh?' said Sanjay, who was staring at Oz. Ellie's twin brother was trying to **balance the footy** on his foot as he hopped along. It wasn't going well.

The footy fell and Sanjay burst out laughing like it was the most **HILARIOUS** thing he'd ever seen.

'Hey!' said Oz, clearly miffed.

Sanjay fell quiet. 'Sorry.'

'So, Sanjay?' asked Ellie as they approached the milkbar. 'This is your **FIRST GRAND FINAL!** We're heading into the Big Dance! That one day in September! Totally awesome, huh?'

Sanjay nodded, though Ellie thought he still looked weirdly distracted. 'Totally.'

'Personally, I can't wait to –'

'Hey, Oz!' Sanjay interrupted. 'Remember the time you stepped in **DOG POO** before training, so I collected what was left and sprinkled it around the ground so no-one would work out the smell was coming from you?'

'Um ... no?' said Oz, **scrunching** up his face. 'Did you really do that?'

'Uh-huh,' said Sanjay with a grin. 'And remember that time a seagull stole a killer python right out of your hand, and I

climbed halfway up the
school flagpole to try
to get it back?'

Oz nodded sadly.
**'WORST DAY
EVER.'**

'And that
time I wore a
Tom Hawkins
mask all
afternoon
so you could pretend you were mates
with him?'

'Hey, as far as I'm concerned that really
WAS Tomahawk!'

Ellie tuned out Sanjay's **Monday morning WEIRDNESS**, her thoughts returning to the Mad Maths Championship letter in her bag.

What if she didn't make the team?

What if all that practice and all those sums meant **NOTHING?**

What if—

'Isn't that right, Ellie?'

Ellie shook off her thoughts. 'Er, sorry?'

Sanjay was bouncing around all over the place. 'Oz and I are **great mates**, aren't we? Always have been.'

Ellie eyed Sanjay uncertainly. 'I guess?'

'Right, Oz?' Sanjay prompted.

'What ... hey, look!' said Oz, pointing at the surf shop. 'They have Falcons t-shirts!'

Oz ran towards the window, SQUISHING his face against it for a closer look.

Sanjay hesitated, his face caught somewhere between **HOPE** and disappointment.

'You right, Sanj?' asked Ellie.

Sanjay barely looked at Ellie before **chasing after** Oz. 'Are you sure they're not chickens?' asked Sanjay, joining Oz at the shop window. 'It doesn't actually say Falcons anywhere.'

'Dude, it's Grand Final week. They've probably had them made specially,' said

Oz, **dragging** Sanjay into the shop.

'You're probably right,' Sanjay agreed. 'You usually are.'

Ellie shook her head, eyeing the t-shirts that were definitely doves, and absolutely **NOT** falcons.

At least this gave her a chance to find out what was in the letter. There was no point putting it off a minute longer. She dug it out of her bag, and ripped it open.

It was a letter of congratulations. **ELLIE WAS IN!**

She took a long minute to calm her racing heart. All that hard work *had* paid off.

Ellie quickly scanned the rest of the letter, which named the other members of the State Team.

And one name leapt out:

JACK PANG.

WHAT?

Ellie read the letter more carefully. There'd been a late withdrawal due to illness, and the back-up replacement for the Squad was Jack Pang.

'What's that?' asked Oz as he bounded out of the shop again.

Ellie **HURLED** the letter into the nearby bin. She *had* to get better at being snuck up on.

'NOTHING!'

'Yeah, right.'

Oz – who was no stranger to a little grossness – stuck his hand in the bin and pulled out the letter. It was covered in **bin juice**, but still clearly readable.

'It's just about that maths thingy you've got. When is that anyway?' he asked casually, not seeming to care about the answer.

Ellie felt that same **rush of anger** she'd been battling the last few days. How could he forget? She'd been talking about it **FOR WEEKS!**

'None of your business!' Ellie snapped, yanking the letter off her brother.

Oz shrugged. 'Fine. Whatever. Now on to more important things.' He waved at Sanjay who was practising his **victory dance** in the reflection from the milkbar window. 'If we hurry, we've got time for a quick practice before school. If we're going to win **THE BIG ONE**, we **HAVE** to beat you-know-who. So, we have to focus entirely on **HIM!**'

'Great idea!' Sanjay agreed, even though his forehead went all crumply. 'Whatever you say, Oz. Want me to carry your bag?'

Ellie watched her annoying brother and suddenly **SUPER WEIRD** cousin hurry off, like nothing else mattered. They didn't even look back to see if Ellie was following.

CHAPTER 5

Sanjay found that the school day **FLEW BY** – Mondays didn't come much better than this! There were **Falcons posters** all around Fresca Bay Primary; Principal Wiley spent the whole assembly talking about the game; and someone got to the sound system, replacing the school bell with the Falcons theme song. The echo of countless *eeeeeeps!* rang in Sanjay's ears all morning.

Being a part of the **Falcons team** made Sanjay feel a bit like a celebrity in the playground. Some parents even showed up to watch training after school. Everyone was **SUPER PUMPED**.

Coach Daisy wore a green, gold and blue suit that she'd had made for the occasion. And every so often she would stop the drills and give a player a random hug. When she got to Sanjay, she added a little electro-shuffle. And she could *dance*. Sanjay **BOOGIED** along with her.

The Falcons finished the training session with drills in each of their zones. Oz was getting **SUPER** bossy in the centre square. At one stage, Sanjay short-passed to Oz, but he was so busy telling Ginger what to do, that the footy hit Oz on the **BUM** with a **THUMP!**

Sanjay's stomach sank.

'Whoops! Sorry!' called Sanjay, as some of the other Falcons laughed. But Oz wasn't listening – he was too busy yelling at Koa to **lift his game**.

Sanjay glanced across the oval to see where Coach Daisy was. She wouldn't be happy seeing Oz lose it like that ...

'**OSCAR LITTLE!**' Coach Daisy's voice rang out across the field. For once, Frankie Falcon, the team mascot, didn't try to copy her.

Daisy stormed over, and Sanjay saw Oz's whole body hunch over.

'**Watch your attitude, Oz,**' Coach Daisy said. Oz just stared at his feet.

Daisy called Ellie over from the forwards' group. 'Now, for the Grand Final we're going to change things up a bit. We're going to play Ellie **in the ruck**.'

'And send me down forward!' said Ginger, fist pumping. 'Awesome!'

'Why?' asked Oz. 'Seems super risky

to make such a **MASSIVE CHANGE** for the Big One!'

'I agree,' said Sanjay, '... and ... Oz's hair looks good!'

Daisy seemed puzzled.

'New gel,' admitted Oz. 'But seriously, is this a good idea?'

''Course,' it is,' said Ellie as she threw a footy in the air and had a go at **tapping it** to Oz. 'And you *know* why.'

Oz caught the footy with a sigh. 'Don't say –'

'– Jumpin' Jack Pang!' said Ellie.

Oz threw down his mouthguard in disgust.

'If he plays, yes,' said Daisy. 'He's the Cockroaches' best ruck. But, no matter who they play there, the Cockroaches are **TALL**. We need Ellie's extra height, *and* her ability to convert **down forward**. Plus, they won't be expecting it.'

Sanjay thought it sounded like a good idea. But Oz had his arms crossed and was all pouty. So, Sanjay did the same.

Daisy sent them into different groups to practise drills.

Sanjay made sure he was in Oz's group, but Oz seemed pretty keen to follow Ellie.

'Okay,' Daisy said, **'let's try some hit outs.'** She pointed to some witches hats she'd set out on the wing.

'I'll be Jack,' Sanjay offered, pulling a demonic face as they set up for the play.

'Hang on, Ellie – I've got an idea!' Oz said. Ellie didn't seem **SUPER KEEN** to hear it. 'What?'

Oz looked fit to burst. 'Remember back when we used to play with ... *him*?'

'The **TRAITOR?**' Sanjay said at the precise moment Ellie said, 'Jumpin' Jack?'

Oz nodded. 'Like I said, *him*.'

Ellie rolled her eyes.

'Remember our signature play, Ellie? No-one could stop us!'

'What play?' Sanjay asked.

'The amazing, spectacular, **TWIN TAKE OFF!**' Oz announced it like Sanjay should know what it meant.

Ellie didn't seem impressed. 'You mean, the one where I'm your decoy and you have all the fun?'

'It's a genius move – worked every time! Even on *you know who!*'

Ellie frowned. 'That was just in practice drills. We never tried it in a real game. Besides, I'm a **BETTER KICK** now. It doesn't make sense anymore.'

'Can't you at least give it a try?' Oz pleaded.

'Daisy won't like it,' Ellie said.

Oz shrugged. 'Daisy won't know ... '
And finally Oz looked at Sanjay. 'Will she,
Sanjay?'

Sanjay's cheeks grew hot. He suspected
this was a **terrible idea**, but there
was no way he could say no to Oz. 'Er, no.
'Course not.'

Ellie looked like she was about to
object, but **fell silent** as their coach
approached them.

'Okay, team. You ready for some drills?'

'We're ready,' Oz said. 'Aren't we, Ellie?'

Sanjay noticed Ellie stiffen, but she
nodded, and everyone took their place.

'You can't start your run up there,'

Oz said, pointing. 'Get back further.'

'I've stepped it out, Oz,' Ellie **SNAPPED**.

Oz stayed quiet but Sanjay was sure he could see his cousin *literally* biting his tongue.

Daisy bounced the ball, and Ellie **EASILY** won the ruck contest against Sanjay – it was like Emma King versus Caleb Daniel! Ellie tapped the ball back to Oz. With an opponent in front of them – Sanjay as Jack – Oz booted the ball high into the sky, way up into the clouds.

Meanwhile, Sanjay noticed Oz **dropping low** and linking his hands together. What was he up to?

Ellie stepped onto Oz's hands and he gave her a boost, just as she jumped.

So, this was the **TWIN TAKE OFF!**

As Ellie flew up into the sky she cried

'Miiiiiiine!'

Sanjay lost sight of the footy and kept his eyes on Ellie as she was calling for the ball. But Oz had put enough length into the kick that he knew exactly where it was headed, and **marked it** a few metres to Sanjay's right! Oz was already in position and heading for goal – Sanjay wouldn't have time to catch him.

'Ozzy rules!' cried Oz. 'Take that!'

But Oz was running out of puff – trying to do too much, Sanjay guessed. His long strides left him off balance and he toppled forward, **FACE FIRST** in the mud.

'I knew it wouldn't work!' Ellie replied with a huff. 'That was such a dumb idea!'

Daisy glanced at the twins, then at Sanjay. 'I'm not sure what just happened, but we need to work together. Cool it with the squabbling, okay?'

Sanjay looked at Oz who was shaking his head. He wanted to say he liked the move, but he didn't want Daisy to hear.

Daisy blew her whistle. **'All right, Falcons, bring it in.'**

All the players gathered around Daisy. There was a lot of jostling and muttering, and everyone seemed a bit on edge. Like Oz's mood had infected everyone.

'Right, kids! Important announcement.'

The team hushed and waited for their coach.

'I know everyone's excited about the **BIG GAME**.'

A chorus of chattering broke out. Sanjay saw Oz hanging back, as though he wasn't so sure.

'It's **SUPER EXCITING ... _BUT_**.' Daisy took a long minute to make eye contact with each and every one of them. 'But,' she said again, her eyes landing on Oz, who squirmed on the spot. 'We need to think like a **TEAM!** It's not about one player. Or who will star. It's about how we work together! That means looking out for each other, helping each other, supporting each other ... ' Daisy's eyes narrowed. 'And _listening_ to each other.'

Sanjay's teammates murmured their agreement, nodding and slapping each other on the back. Sanjay patted Oz on the back, but Oz didn't seem to notice.

'Most of all – we want to have **FUN!**'

The Falcons all **CHEERED**, stomping their feet and clapping.

'So, we're all agreed?' Coach Daisy said when they quieted. She didn't name Oz specifically, but even Sanjay could tell that's who she was talking to.

Everyone else seemed to know too, because Sanjay's teammates all looked at Oz.

Without even thinking, Sanjay's hand

shot up. 'I agree with Oz,' he announced.

'Thank you, Sanjay,' Coach Daisy said dryly. 'Except he hasn't said anything yet.'

'Oh.' A knot formed in Sanjay's throat. He swallowed. 'Well, I just know he'll be right.'

Ellie shot him a **puzzled** look, while the rest of his teammates looked like they might laugh.

Sanjay's cheeks burned. He glanced at his cousin to make sure he'd heard. Sanjay didn't like being embarrassed, but being a best mate sometimes meant doing **EMBARRASSING** things.

After training, Sanjay followed Oz up to their classroom. 'Hey dude, can I teach you my victory dance for Saturday now?'

Oz was studying the ground as they walked. 'What?'

'It's like a **shuffle** meets the **floss** with a couple of **dabs** thrown in. I call it a Floffle-Dab!'

But Oz didn't seem to be listening. He stopped walking, but barely looked up. Panicking, Sanjay blurted out, 'I can do the **TWIN TAKE OFF** with you instead! Since Ellie doesn't want to.'

Oz frowned, like Sanjay had lost his

mind. 'What? No. We've been doing it for **YEARS**. You have to *really* know someone to trust them like that. You can't just learn it in a few days. It takes **FOREVER**.'

'Oh. Right,' Sanjay said, his heart sinking. 'Understood.'

As Sanjay watched his cousin disappearing into the classroom, head down, all small and quiet, Sanjay realised he would **NEVER** catch up in the best friend race. Not to Ellie, of course. But not even to Jack.

And he couldn't help wondering – were he and Oz *actually* best friends after all?

CHAPTER

6

Oz went to bed Tuesday night with less of a tingly feeling from the top of his head to the tips of his toes ... and more a sinking feeling **DEEP IN HIS GUT**. The last few days hadn't just been a rollercoaster. They'd been an **OUT-OF-CONTROL** rollercoaster that was speeding through a volcano and headed for a hurricane.

Grand Final week was **FULL ON**. Mostly because Oz had always loved winning. Who didn't, right? And **GRAND FINALS** were the **BEST** kind of winning. This was the **BIGGEST WEEK** of his life!

But no-one seemed to care anywhere near as much as they should! Even Coach Daisy was worried about them "having fun", when they should be focused on trying to **WIN**.

Wasn't that the whole point of footy?

But Oz couldn't help feeling that *maybe* it was less about winning the

Grand Final with the Falcons, and more about beating Jumpin' Jack Pang once and for all. To really teach him a lesson for betraying their team and **betraying** Oz.

Because moving schools, changing teams, starting a whole new life **WAS** a kind of betrayal, wasn't it?

It sure felt like it to Oz.

It didn't help that Ellie and Sanjay were acting **SUPER** strange. Sanjay was normally a pretty helpful dude, but he was being **SO** helpful that he almost … wasn't? Oz didn't know *what* was going on with Sanjay, but he seemed to agree with everything Oz said – even before he said it! And during lunchtime, Sanjay had offered to 'pre-chew' Oz's bubble gum for him. Things were getting **WEIRD**.

Ellie was no better. Oz had no idea what was wrong with his sister, but Ellie was barely talking to him! She had her head in her maths books twenty-four seven, and any time Oz tried to get her to practise the **TWIN TAKE OFF**, she'd get angry all over again, like *he'd* done something wrong.

Ellie wouldn't even listen to Oz at training when he tried to help her! She'd never match the Cockroaches' gameplay if she didn't focus. And acing some dumb maths test was **NOT** going to help the Falcons on the weekend.

The Grand Final was all that mattered. The **BIG ONE!**

Why was **HE** the only one who seemed to get that?

Oz rolled onto his side. Then a few seconds later he rolled the other way. The pillow felt hot and lumpy. He kicked away the sheets. **PUNCHED** his pillow. Then rolled over on to his back. But no matter what he did, his eyes wouldn't stay closed.

He flicked on his light, yanked on his Geelong dressing gown and his cat-eared slippers, and wandered into the kitchen.

Luke was already awake, and **cooking up a storm**. At least Oz would have time for an extra breakfast.

'You're up early!' Luke said, as he put a tray of something gloopy into the oven. (It may have looked gloopy, but it smelt **DELICIOUS!**)

Oz shrugged. He started to take a muffin from a tray on the bench, but Luke slapped his hand away.

'Give it a minute, mate! They're still steaming.'

WORTH A TRY.

'Too excited to sleep, hey?' Luke said, waving the muffin around to cool it down.

Oz shrugged. He couldn't sleep, but he wasn't sure this feeling was **excitement**. 'I guess.'

'Grand Final time can be overwhelming,' said Luke. 'I should know, I've lost count of the catering orders for this week!' He waved his hand at the food spread from end to end. 'I don't even know how I'll manage the Pangs' party on top of all this!'

Oz felt a nasty tug in his chest at the

mention of Jack's family. **UGH!** Why did it feel like this every time he heard his name? Oz reached for another muffin, certain it would make him **feel better**, but Luke stuck a banana in his hand instead. 'This should tide you over.'

'Um, Dad?' said Oz as he unpeeled the banana. 'How do you stop getting side-tracked by ...' Oz wanted to say 'by ex-bffs with mad footy skillz', but instead he said, '... *distractions*.'

Luke stopped stirring and caught Oz's eye. 'It's a **WILD WEEK**, isn't it? Hard to concentrate on the game.'

Oz nodded as he squished the whole

banana into his mouth, filling both cheeks with mush.

'You know what helps me?' asked Luke. 'I get **back to basics**. Try to remember why I love what I do in the first place. That helps me focus. Know what I mean?'

Oz nodded yes, but they both knew he meant *no*.

'What's the most fun bit about footy?' said Luke.

'WINNING!' Oz said.

Luke laughed. 'Fair enough. Anything else?'

'KICKING GOALS?' Oz offered.

'Also good.' Oz's dad grabbed a spatula

to scrape the extra flour and butter from the top of the bowl, mixing all the ingredients together. 'But I think there's **more**. Take these muffins – see how I have to mix the ingredients together to make the batter? None of the ingredients are enough on their own.' He grinned. 'It's the same with footy.'

'Okay ...'

'It's the whole team,' Luke prompted.

Oz frowned. This sounded an awful lot like what Coach Daisy was saying.

'So, apart from winning and kicking goals, is there anything about footy that you love most of all?' Luke set the batter down and waited.

It was suddenly completely clear to Oz what his dad was saying. '**THE FALCONS!** Playing with the other kids.'

'*Exactly.*'

Oz nodded. Little bits of banana dripped onto the bench as he swallowed it down with a big gulp. It was hard to talk, so he just pointed at the muffin. Surely it was cool enough now?

His dad laughed. 'All right. Just one.'

Oz stuffed the muffin in his mouth, tasting all the yumminess mixed together to make this perfect delicious thing.

Dad was right. So was Coach Daisy. Teamwork was the best part of footy.

Which was **EXACTLY** what made the **TWIN TAKE OFF** so awesome! Ellie and Oz had to work together to do the **OTHER** most fun thing there was – **WINNING!**

And that meant beating Jack Pang!

CHAPTER

7

Ellie sighed. She couldn't believe the words coming out of her brother's mouth, even when he repeated himself.

'You heard correctly. I'll be holding an **EXTRA TRAINING SESSION** tomorrow after school,' said Oz.

'Great idea, Oz. I'm in!' said Sanjay, with

two thumbs up.

Coach Daisy was up on the slope that led to the oval, chatting **tactics** with Principal Wiley while the Falcons packed up their gear after their training session. Everyone was puffed. They'd trained well. In fact, everyone had put in 110 per cent because it was meant to be their **last training** before the Grand Final – but it wasn't enough for Oz.

'This is the Grand Final, guys! We need to be ready!' Oz cried. 'And we *will* be ready or my name isn't **OSCAR CORNELIUS LITTLE!**'

Most Falcons grunted in agreement

as they continued putting away cones, training goals and crash mats. But a couple sniggered at *Cornelius*.

'I expect to see everyone here this time tomorrow.' Oz locked eyes on Ellie.

Ellie **HURLED** down a couple of witches hats and crossed her arms.

'Ellie, you look like you're holding in gas,' whispered Rana. 'Should I move away?'

'No. It's just Oz being ... well, *Oz*.'

'Yeah,' said Rana. 'But I guess an **extra training session** can't hurt. Even if it's not Coach Daisy's idea.'

'It's not that,' said Ellie turning to Rana. 'I can't come to the extra training sesh.'

'Oh yeah – the **MAD MATHS CHAMPIONSHIP!**' said Rana.

'Exactly.' Ellie straightened one of the witches hats to make it line up just right. 'But **OF COURSE** Oz is so **OBSESSED** with beating the Cockroaches that he's **COMPLETELY FORGOTTEN** about it.'

'Really?' Rana frowned. 'Are you sure?'

Ellie shrugged. 'Why else would he organise extra training when I can't come?' She squinted at the row of witches hats, shifting one just so. 'He knows Mad Maths is a big deal to me. But he doesn't care at all.'

'Bummer,' said Rana. 'I know it's the

Grand Final. But Mad Maths is pretty huge too.'

'**RIGHT?**' Ellie didn't mean to shout at Rana, but at least her friend understood.

Footy was definitely one of the most important things in Ellie's life. And she'd do **ANYTHING** for the team. But she'd committed to the Mad Maths Squad ages ago. Plus, she **LOVED** maths! Oz would never understand, but it was true.

Winning the Championship was as important to Ellie as winning the **GRAND FINAL**.

Which was why she'd invited Jack to practise with her that night after school.

Her dad had sorted it out with Jack's parents. Ellie thought about how Oz would react, and immediately felt a twist in her belly. If Oz knew she was hanging out with Jack Pang, he would **COMPLETELY FREAK OUT**.

Then again, what Oz didn't know couldn't hurt him – Ellie had overheard his plans to stay behind at school and talk GF tactics with Ginger.

Besides, she decided, **bristling** inside. It was none of his business! Oz wasn't even interested in the Mad Maths Squad – and she was allowed to be friends with whoever she wanted.

'So, what are you gonna tell Oz about the training session?' Rana asked.

'I'll tell him the truth,' Ellie said, more bravely than she felt. 'That I have other plans!'

Jumpin' Jack Pang had grown even taller than Ellie remembered. And the guy seemed to look musclier than ever! **NO WONDER** Oz was so worried about beating him on the weekend.

'Hey Jack! Thanks for coming.'

Jack **grinned**, ducking his head even though he *probably* wouldn't have hit the doorjamb.

'Hey Ellie. Thanks for inviting me! I need all the practise I can get!'

Ellie nodded, thinking how **TRICKY** the Championship was going to be with a replacement player. But she didn't want to make Jack feel bad, so she said, **'You'll be fine! No big deal.'**

Jack just grinned again.

Ellie led Jack through to her room, telling him her plan for the contest as they went.

She was setting out notepaper filled with **rows of sums**, when she realised Jack had barely spoken a word.

'Sorry I keep going on,' Ellie said. 'I'm just

super excited about the Championship.'
She blushed a little. 'And nervous, too.'

Jack glanced back toward Ellie's
doorway, a **FUNNY FROWN** on his
face. 'It's cool ... I was just ... checking who
else is here?'

Ellie's stomach dropped. Of course he
meant Oz, and *of course* Jack was going
to feel weird! Oz completely bailed on Jack
after he changed teams. Her brother had
made up excuses, but Jack had to have
known why Oz **cut him off**.

Ellie smiled gently. 'You worried about
Oz?'

Jack shrugged. 'I don't really know

why. But he was so weird after I left. And I haven't really seen him since. I guess I was away for a while ...' But Jack's face was all scrunched up, and Ellie was pretty sure he didn't believe that was the problem.

'But you're here now, right? And we can **hang out again**, like we used to.'

'That would be great! I'm super pumped about the contest, but a bit nervous as well. Especially since I thought I'd miss out.'

'I'm pumped too. It's just cool to finally hang with someone who likes numbers the way I do.'

'TOTALLY!'

They were halfway through a tricky

multiplication problem when Ellie heard Oz's voice in the kitchen.

And suddenly her decision not to tell him about Jack seemed like a *really* bad plan.

She was just about to warn Jack, when her brother appeared in the doorway. Oz's expression turned to stone.

'What is **THE TRAITOR** doing here?'

Ellie was too shocked to respond. She knew Oz would be mad, but she had no idea he'd be so **RUDE!**

Jack's face fell. 'What did you call me?' His voice was quiet.

Ellie glared at her brother, fury hot in her throat. '**OSCAR LITTLE! MIND**

YOUR MANNERS!'

But Oz wasn't listening. He couldn't seem to look at Jack anymore – his eyes drilled into Ellie instead.

'HOW COULD YOU?!' Oz yelled, throwing his arms up.

'How could *I*?' Ellie shouted back.

Jack looked genuinely startled. 'I didn't mean to cause trouble,' he said, his brow crinkled in confusion, and what Ellie realised was sadness. **'I'd better go,'** he added, not waiting for either of them to answer as he bolted out of the room.

Ellie was frozen in mute fury. She couldn't think of a single thing to say that would explain all the things she was feeling.

Oz and Ellie both **GLARED** at each other for a long moment.

Finally, Ellie found her voice. 'Jack was visiting **ME!**' she replied. 'He's **MY** friend! I'm allowed to have my own friends, you know!'

'Just tell me one thing,' Oz growled. Did you tell him about our plan?'

'What in the **WORLD** are you talking about?'

Oz's eyes were so wide, Ellie thought they'd pop right out of his head. '**THE TWIN TAKE OFF**, of course!'

Ellie opened her mouth, about to protest about **EVERYTHING**, when Sanjay appeared in the doorway.

'Hey guys ...' He looked nervous, and just *weird* – even weirder than he had been lately, which was a *lot*. 'Is everything okay?'

'Perfectly fine, Sanj,' Ellie said

sarcastically. 'As long as I let Oz run my life! Including who I'm friends with, what I do in my spare time, and even **HOW I PLAY FOOTBALL!**' Ellie faced Oz, heat in her cheeks. 'I'm not interested in your stupid game plan and your stupid **TWIN TAKE OFF!**'

'You promised, Ellie!' Oz yelled.

'No, I didn't! But you wouldn't know, because you haven't been listening! You don't care what I want! It's all about **YOU!**'

'Maybe we could come up with a different move, Oz?' Sanjay said, his voice a bit shaky. 'Something just as awesome –'

Oz barely looked at Sanjay. 'We spent **YEARS** perfecting the **TWIN TAKE OFF**. It's the only way to beat **THE TRAITOR!**'

Sanjay seemed to shrink before Ellie's eyes.

'Don't worry, Sanjay,' she said. 'Oz has lost his mind!' She put her arm around her cousin. 'Maybe after the weekend, the **REAL** Oz will come back. Because this one is **SUPER ANNOYING**.'

Oz seemed to puff up with rage. 'You won't work with me on our signature move – our one hope to win on Saturday! You're doing **MATHS** instead of preparing for the game. **AND**, you're hanging out with my **ARCH ENEMY!** You're meant to be on my side!' he shouted. 'You're my twin sister, remember?'

Ellie shook her head, her cheeks burning. **'HOW COULD I EVER FORGET!'**

'Then **ACT** like it!' Oz shouted.

And with that, he turned on his heel and left.

Later, after a painfully quiet dinner where Luke kept asking them what was wrong, and Oz and Ellie refused to answer, Luke finally hit on the problem as they were clearing the table. 'Did I see Jack Pang heading down Shepherd Court before dinner? Preparation for tomorrow, El?'

Ellie glanced at her brother. 'Yep.'

'**Nice boy**, that one.' Luke set his dishes down. 'Leave you to it, kids.'

The moment their dad disappeared, Oz turned to Ellie.

'Tomorrow?' asked Oz. 'You're seeing **THE TRAITOR *AGAIN*?**' And then, as though he'd just realised, his face fell. 'Hang on – we have the special training session tomorrow!'

'I'm not coming,' Ellie said evenly. 'I'm going to the Mad Maths Championship instead.' She stood a little taller, bracing herself. 'If you weren't so selfish, you would have remembered that!'

'But we need to practise the **TWIN TAKE OFF!**'

Ellie gritted her teeth. 'Not tomorrow.'

'You're choosing *maths* over the Falcons?' Oz almost spat the word 'maths' like it tasted gross in his mouth.

Ellie tried to keep her voice steady. 'It's not about choosing one over the other.'

Oz seemed to think about that for a moment before he frowned. 'What's **JACK PANG** got to do with your stupid maths test?'

Ellie could ignore Oz calling the **Championship** a "test". And she could **IGNORE** the fact that he called it "stupid". But she wouldn't ignore how mean he was being about Jack.

'First of all, Jack Pang is in my Maths Squad.'

Oz blinked.

'And second of all, Jack Pang was *my* friend, too. Not just *yours*. And he still **IS** my friend. I don't know **WHY** I let you tell me otherwise.'

Oz's face had turned **beetroot red**. His mouth moved for a full minute before any words came out, but Ellie could see the rage bubbling anyway.

'Fine,' Oz finally said through a clenched jaw. 'You do what you have to do. Good luck!'

'Thanks. I will,' Ellie barked back.

Oz glared at her for a long minute. 'But if we lose on Saturday, **IT'S ON YOU**.'

The next night, Ellie and Rana were standing outside the Convention Centre exit where the Mad Maths Championship had just been held, waiting for Ellie's dad to collect them. In Ellie's hand was a **HUGE** trophy. And on her face was a

HUGE SMILE. In fact, she was grinning so much her cheeks were hurting.

'This is the coooolest!' said Rana. 'Congratulations again, Ellie! That was **AAAAAHMAZING**.'

'Thanks for coming. Sorry if Oz was weird about you missing training. He should really be here as well.'

Rana shrugged. 'Thought you were sick of doing everything together?'

'I am. But that doesn't mean he shouldn't support me when it matters. Today was **MY** thing. It would have been cool if he'd come to watch.'

'True. I'm glad *I* was here,' said Rana.

'You're a **DEADSET CHAMPION!** Like the Dusty Martin of maths, I reckon.'

Ellie blushed. 'Thanks, Rana. But I think that's the twentieth time you've said that.'

'Well, I **REALLY** mean it!' said Rana. 'Your team **SMASHED IT!** And it was great to see Jack Pang again. Do you reckon he's got even *taller* since he left Fresca Bay?'

Ellie laughed. 'Seems like it. Though I'm surprised he showed up after everything that happened with Oz yesterday.' Ellie had told Rana about how **HORRIBLE** Oz had been.

'Hey, Ellie!' Jack said, coming out of the Convention Centre. He held up his own trophy. 'How cool is this?'

'It's **AWESOME!**'

'Congratulations, Jack!' Rana said. 'But I hope that's your last trophy for the week,' she added with a grin.

Jack laughed. 'Who knows? The Grand Final will be **HUGE** either way.'

Just then, Ellie spotted her dad driving up in the minivan, with Oz and Sanjay in the back seat.

Ellie could feel Oz's **hot glare** through the car window.

'That's my cousin, Sanjay,' Ellie said, pointing him out to Jack.

Ellie noticed Sanjay's wide-eyed stare through the window. He'd been **SO WEIRD** lately. Different weird to Oz, but still weird. Ellie was starting to wonder if this whole Grand Final thing was going to be as much fun as she'd thought.

Sanjay was staring at Jack. He opened his mouth like he was about to speak, but then stopped. Ellie couldn't be sure, but she thought she saw Oz give him a nudge.

'Well, **CONGRATULATIONS** again, Jack!' Ellie said.

'You too!'

'See you on Saturday!' she called out as they all piled into the van.

As they drove off, Rana turned to Ellie. 'He's even taller up close,' she said, pulling a scary face. 'We're going to need **LOTS** of luck on Saturday!'

Oz's grumpy *HRMPH!* was all the answer anyone needed.

CHAPTER

8

Sanjay stayed up late on Grand Final eve.

Oz had seemed distracted during the extra training session on Thursday, and even Sanjay tried to come up with some other ideas – some **SUPER**, **AWESOME** moves – but Oz wasn't impressed **AT ALL**.

And that *stung*. Sanjay was starting to wonder where he fit in Oz's world. The only thing he was sure about was that the Grand Final would make all the difference. He was **DETERMINED** to show his commitment to Oz and the Falcons. He just had to work out how.

After talking with his Uncle Luke, Sanjay had a **BRILLIANT** idea!

He would bake **SUPER HIGH ENERGY** protein bars to give the team the extra boost they'd need to take on the Cockroaches. Or, at least, to take on Jumpin' Jack Pang.

The more he thought about it, the

more excited Sanjay got! Not only did it mean he'd be helping Oz and the Falcons win, but it was also the **BEST** way to win over Oz – through his stomach!

Sanjay spent the evening baking the **PERFECT BATCH**. He found it kind of calming, actually – working through the ingredients, rolling and sifting and mixing. The recipe said it was best to eat them right before exercise, so he planned to hand them out to the team as a surprise **just before the game**.

He'd laid the bars out on the bench to cool overnight, and the next morning he was trying to find a container to put them in when he heard a **LOUD GROAN** from the downstairs toilet.

Soon after, Sanjay's dad came staggering out of the bathroom, his face grey as dishwater.

'You all right, Dad?'

Lenny offered a weak grin. 'Bit of **tummy trouble**. Probably shouldn't have had that midnight snack. No worries, though. I'll be good for the game.' The words had barely left his mouth before he **BOLTED** back to the toilet.

Sanjay's mum, Prishna, came in, Bela and Charu in tow, all of them dressed and ready to go.

Sanjay couldn't wait to get to the game and see Oz's face when he showed him the **MAGIC, SUPER-POWERED** energy bars. That's **EXACTLY** the sort of commitment Oz would approve of. BFF material for sure!

'Ready to go, Sanj?' Prishna asked.

'What about Dad?'

Prishna offered a lopsided grin at the **GROSS** noises coming from the toilet. 'I think he'll have to meet us there. He can pick up Aahna from Ben's house on the way.'

As Sanjay **hurried** through the gathering crowd at the oval on his way to the change rooms, he saw Principal Wiley and Manny from the milkbar making last minute preparations on the banners. Mrs Tan and Ms Miffy-Osborne were hanging streamers and balloons, and some year six kids were setting up a spot to sell footy records.

Sanjay was so excited, he started dancing outside the change rooms.

It was **FINALLY** here. The **GRAND FINAL! THE BIG ONE!** All year the Falcons had worked for this – sometimes it was all Oz and Ellie talked about – and now, they'd **actually made it**.

Sanjay clung to the container of energy bars, dying to tell Oz what he'd been working on.

The minute he saw his Uncle Luke's minivan pull up, he raced over to meet them.

'Sanjay!' Uncle Luke called out. **'Excited, mate?'**

Sanjay performed the Cupid Shuffle, finishing it off with a mini-pirouette. His uncle laughed out loud.

Ellie clapped. 'I think that's a **YES!**'

Oz and Ellie joined Sanjay, their gear slung over their shoulders.

'Where's Uncle Lenny?' Ellie asked.

Prishna winked at Sanjay. 'He'll be along a little later. He's not feeling the best right now – bit of a **tummy bug**.'

'Not another midnight snack?' Luke asked.

The whole family chuckled. Sanjay's dad was famous for eating **too much** at all the wrong times.

Suddenly, Sanjay's grin faded.

MIDNIGHT SNACK!

What if ...?

He carefully opened the container of energy bars and showed them to Oz.

'I made these **SUPER-POWERED**

energy bars for the team, to give us an extra boost.'

Oz whistled, nodding. 'They look **great**, Sanj!'

But that gnawing feeling wouldn't ease. Sanjay had made exactly one for each Falcon. He started counting the bars, his stomach dropping as he got near the end.

There was one missing.

'UH OH.'

'What's up?' Oz asked.

Everyone looked at Sanjay. Even Oz seemed to focus for a moment.

'I think Dad ate one of them.' Sanjay swallowed loudly. 'I think that's what **made him sick**.'

Luke frowned. 'Are you sure? Did you follow the recipe?'

Sanjay went through the list of ingredients – he'd memorised the lot. '... and four cups of fibre powder.'

Luke's eyes grew wide. 'Four *cups* of fibre powder?'

Sanjay nodded, **DREAD** growing in the pit of his stomach.

Luke cleared his throat. 'I'm pretty sure it would've said four *teaspoons* of fibre powder.'

Prishna seemed to be trying not to laugh, but Sanjay's stomach **lurched**.

Luke shook his head, the edge of a smile on his lips. 'He'll be fine, Sanjay. But that explains his, er, bathroom issues.'

'Enough **mucking about**,' said Oz, pointing to the change rooms. 'Let's focus.'

'Yes, sir! snapped Ellie, earning a dark look from Oz.

'I'll deal with these,' Sanjay muttered, taking a detour to the rows of industrial bins on the other side of the change rooms. A few of the Cockroaches players were filing into their change rooms, **bumping** and **jostling** each other with that same mix of excitement and nerves Sanjay had felt only moments before.

'Hey – it's Sanjay, right?'

Sanjay looked up to see **Jumpin' Jack Pang** heading towards him.

'Hey. Um, yeah … Jack …?'

Sanjay glanced over his shoulder. He wasn't super keen for Oz to see him talking to Jack. But Jack was also Ellie's friend. Sanjay was totally confused. It was kind of hard to think of Jack as a traitor. He just seemed like a normal kid. **A pretty cool one, actually**.

'What have you got there?'

Sanjay opened the container. 'They're

energy bars. I made them for the team. They didn't quite work. I was about to throw them out.' At least that was true.

'They look great to me! I could do with one of those right now.' And before Sanjay could protest, Jack grabbed a power bar and was about to stick it in his mouth.

'NO! WAIT!' Sanjay yelped.

Mouth open, Jack stopped.

For a long moment, Sanjay debated what to say.

The truth was, he wasn't **COMPLETELY** certain that an energy bar had made his dad sick. Maybe it didn't? His dad was **ALWAYS** sneaking off for midnight feasts. Maybe he'd eaten a block of chocolate all by himself? Or a bag of liquorice?

Sanjay cleared his throat. 'They're best eaten **right before the game**.'

Jack grinned. 'Cool! Thanks, mate.' And he headed to the change rooms, clutching the dodgy energy bar like a treasure.

Sanjay watched Jack leave, the word "STOP!" stuck somewhere at the back of his throat. The twist in his belly tightened, but it was like his feet were glued to the spot.

Whether Jack really was a traitor or not, he was an **AMAZING** player. If they could keep Jack quiet, like Oz said, maybe that would be enough to help the Falcons win. And if the Falcons won, **everyone** would be happy. Especially Oz!

So Sanjay stood there in painful silence, and let Jack walk away.

CHAPTER

9

The Falcons burst out onto the ground. The crowd **ROARED** as their theme song played, and Ellie stole a moment to just **take it all in**.

The grandstand was **PACKED!** You could feel the excitement in the air. There were so many faces they all blurred into one. Kids, adults, dogs, and Frankie, the cockie who thought he was a falcon, had all turned out to see the big game.

Ellie clapped and **CHEERED**, making it her mission to set the team's mood. This was Grand Final Day after all – everyone deserved a bit of a pump-up. Plus, she was still super hyped from winning the **Mad Maths Championship**. Imagine if they won today, too!

'Here comes Koa!'

'Look out, it's Clara the Cat!'

'Chiara! Paolo! Bring it in! Woot, woot!'

Ellie jogged over to Rana who was talking to Olivia and Freddo.

'**Let me at 'em!**' said Rana, making a scary face in the direction of the Cockroaches' change room.

Ellie laughed nervously.

'You're not **FREAKING OUT**, are ya?' asked Rana. 'Come on, we'll roast those roaches!'

'Yeah, yeah. I know. It's just ... they beat us this year by **A MILE**. And now they have Jack ... ' Ellie leant in to whisper, in case Oz overheard them. 'Even *The Coastal Times* said they'd be unstoppable with Jack back!'

'Pfft. Doesn't scare me,' said Rana, miming a **roundhouse kick** and a one-two punch before setting in her taekwondo **FIGHT POSE**.

Ellie laughed. 'I believe you!'

Ellie noticed Sanjay watching the crowd, and jogged over to him.

'This is **cool**,' said Sanjay. 'I mean, we probably could've done without the butcher's shop staff doing a cheer routine. But the brass band was actually pretty good.'

'Even with Principal Wiley on tuba?'

'He **nailed it**. Till his moustache got caught.'

Ellie and Sanjay looked around at the crowd. The oval was **PACKED**. There were cars on the grassy slope and not a spare seat in the grandstand. The whole of **Fresca Bay** and Colburton must've been there.

Ellie felt Sanjay's eyes on her. 'You okay, Sanj?'

Sanjay blinked. Then shook his head. Then nodded. He opened his mouth like he was about to say something **REALLY IMPORTANT**, but then he closed it.

'All good.'

'Are you sure?'

Sanjay shook his head. 'I'm fine.' He

managed a thin smile. 'I better go see if Oz needs a hand with anything.'

'Really? Um, okay … it's just that … you've been helping Oz a lot lately?'

Sanjay did that weird flapping thing with his mouth again, but still nothing came out. **'Better go!'** he said finally, and headed over to the others.

Ellie shook her head, not sure what to make of her cousin's **WEIRDNESS**.

Coach Daisy was by the bench. She'd gestured Ellie over as she started shuffling the magnets around on her little whiteboard.

'You've got the height and the skill to

match it with the Roaches' ruck. As we all know, Jack's a pretty decent player.'

Ellie laughed to herself. Saying Jumpin' Jack Pang was a **"pretty decent player"** was like saying the twins' father was an "okay cook".

'You know how he plays. You know his strengths – and you know his weaknesses,' said Coach Daisy. 'Use all that knowledge to your **ADVANTAGE**.'

Ellie nodded, her head spinning.

Oz had warned her that if they lost, it would be on her. Since she was starting on Jack, Oz was kind of right. If the Cockroaches got an *early jump* on the

Falcons like last time, it would be, as her Uncle Lenny liked to say, *All over, red rover*. It really *would* be on her!

All of a sudden, Ellie felt as sick as her uncle.

CHAPTER 10

Oz had an electric eel feeling as the Falcons ran a few drills on the edge of the centre square – all wiggly and **BUZZING** as Coach Daisy revved everyone up.

Then the Cockroaches song began, and the opposition players emerged from the visitors' change rooms. They were all

SO TALL. They were met with a **HUGE** cheer – the loudest cheer saved for their star, Jumpin' Jack.

Oz wanted to pretend he hadn't noticed Jack, but he couldn't look away. He was the tallest player in his team, probably the tallest in their league. And he was **BULGING** with actual muscles. Was it possible he'd had another growth spurt just that week? He was **TWICE the size** he was when he played for the Falcons, and he was already tall back then. Dressed in the Cockroaches kit as he ran out onto the oval, Jack looked like an **AFL ruck star** in the making. The next Nic Nat!

Oz watched, mesmerised, as Jack kicked a footy to himself. It was like he had a yo-yo on a string.

And then, as if he could sense him watching, Jack looked **STRAIGHT** at Oz.

OZ FROZE.

But Jack just gave a little nod and started some **drills** with his teammates.

The announcer – who sounded a lot like Manny from the milkbar – asked

everyone to stand for the National
Anthem. As both teams lined up in the
centre, Oz gave Sanjay a nudge when
Lenny and Prishna entered the field.
Both had a mic in their hands.

'**Oh no,**' Sanjay muttered.

Oz grimaced, remembering
what Sanjay had told him
about Lenny's toilet disaster
that morning.

'Is he going to be
okay?' Oz asked.

Sanjay **crossed his
fingers** on both hands
and held them up.

The backing track kicked in. But Lenny and Prishna **BELTED OUT** what turned out to be a rousing rendition of *Advance Australia Fair*. And Lenny didn't fart once – at least not loud enough for the microphone to pick up, which Sanjay and Oz agreed was a **good omen** for the game.

The song ended with another cheer from the crowd, and then each team formed a **HUDDLE**.

But Oz wasn't listening to Coach Daisy or Frankie Falcon. He spent the whole time sneaking glances at Jack over in the Cockroaches' huddle.

What was he planning? How can I stop him? Oz thought.

'Eeeeeeeeeep!' the Falcons all yelled, and Oz joined in. Then they raced to their positions, and Oz watched his sister lining up in the ruck. If she wasn't being super annoying, he might've wished her good luck.

Oh, what the heck.

Oz ran over to Ellie.

'Good luck against the **TRAITOR!**'

Ellie stood **very tall**, and Oz was reminded why she was so good in the ruck.

'Jack is **NOT** a traitor! He used to

be your friend.' Her whole face was twisted and red.

Why did she keep taking Jack's side? What sort of twin was she?

The kind who was pretty cool and a lot of fun, the voice in Oz's head reminded him.

'Just promise me you didn't tell him about the **Twin Take Off**.'

Ellie looked genuinely hurt. 'Do you really think I would?'

For a second, Oz didn't know what to say. The truth was, he was so confused and angry, he didn't know **WHAT** he thought. The only thing he was sure of was that he hated fighting with his sister.

'Just ... **focus on the game**,' said
Oz. 'When it's time for the Twin Take Off,
be ready!'

Ellie stared at Oz for a long moment,
then nodded stiffly before running to the
centre.

Oz took his position at the edge of the
centre square, his belly **wound tight**
like a fist.

CHAPTER
11

The siren sounded, and the umpire in the centre raised the ball in the air as another cheer swept around the oval. All around Sanjay, the Falcons looked steely-eyed, jumping on the spot, eager to get started.

But not Sanjay.

This was meant to be his most

important game ever! But instead, Sanjay's mind was focussed on fibre. Specifically, the extra fibre in the energy bars he'd made. And now, Jack Pang had eaten one.

One minute he was ready to tell Jack the truth about the **dodgy bars**, and the next, he thought of Oz's face. How impressed he'd be once he knew. Sanjay knew how badly Oz wanted to win – almost as much as he wanted to beat Jack! **It wasn't *cheating* exactly**, Sanjay had decided. He didn't *mean* for him to take the energy bar. Jack had helped himself without even asking!

The ball was bounced, and Jack won

the tap easily against Ellie. He flicked the ball over to a Cockroach on the wing, who thumped the ball hard, but it shot off the side of his boot and **TUMBLED** to the boundary, over the line.

Jack seemed fine. And as the game continued, Sanjay had to admit he was playing well. **REALLY** well. Maybe they really were **SUPER-POWERED ENERGY BARS**.

And his dad was obviously feeling better – his performance of the National Anthem proved that.

But the more Sanjay thought about it, the **WORSE** he felt.

When the **quarter time** siren sounded, Sanjay couldn't take it any longer. He was heading for the Cockroaches huddle when Oz called out to him.

'Where are you going, Sanj?' Oz said, running over.

Sanjay was about to explode, he felt **SO GUILTY**. Before he could change his mind, he blurted out the whole story.

Oz's eyes grew wide. His mouth fell open. He glanced over at the Cockroaches huddle, and seemed to think hard about what to do.

'I have to tell him, Oz,' Sanjay said. **'It's cheating.'**

Oz frowned. 'Cheating is when you **betray your team** and play for someone else.'

'Er, well, is it? I'm not sure.'

Oz clapped Sanjay on the back and shrugged. 'It's **TOO LATE** anyway, right? He would have already eaten it.'

Sanjay's whole body slumped. That was true. There was nothing Sanjay could do now except say sorry.

'We've got this, Sanj!' Oz said, with the first **real grin** Sanjay had seen on his face for days. 'Let's go!'

Sanjay should've felt great at putting that smile on Oz's face, but somehow, he managed to play even worse in the second quarter than the first. He couldn't focus. Every time Jack got the ball – which was a lot – Sanjay's gut churned, as he searched for any sign that Jack was feeling sick.

But so far, Sanjay was the only sick one. By halftime, he was racked with guilt. He **couldn't do it**. Even if it meant losing Oz, Sanjay had to tell the truth.

As the siren sounded, Sanjay ran straight for Jack, ignoring Oz on the way.

'Hey Sanjay – thanks for that energy bar!'

Sanjay **cringed**. 'I'm sorry – I shouldn't have given it to you.'

Jack blushed a little. 'It was really nice of you, but I didn't eat it.'

Sanjay was so relieved he could cry! **'You didn't? How come?'**

'To be honest, I forgot! I was nervous when the game started. I was going to have it now, actually.' He flashed Sanjay a grin. 'Get a surge for the second half.'

Sanjay shook his head. '**DON'T!** Please don't eat it.' His cheeks were already warm from the game, but they became as hot as volcanoes now. 'I think there's something **wrong** with them.' He swallowed noisily. 'My dad got sick from having one.'

'SICK?'

'Both ends.'

'Whoa. Wow. Okay. Thanks!' Jack's grin grew wider. 'That's pretty cool of you to tell me. It would have been pretty messy **– SUPER MESSY –** if you hadn't!'

Sanjay hesitated, tempted to leave it there. He glanced up and saw Oz staring at him, the frown clear as day. No. He had to do the right thing, *finally*. 'The truth is, I knew before.' He dropped his head, the weight of it like a stone. 'I should never have let you take one.'

Sanjay waited for Jack to lose his mind, knowing he deserved it.

Instead, Jack laughed. And **LAUGHED**.
Sanjay looked up, shocked. 'It was a
terrible thing to do!'

'I mean, I *did* just grab one without asking,' Jack said, still laughing.

'But ... but ...'

Jack clapped Sanjay on the back. 'Don't worry about it. **All good**.' Then he leant in to Sanjay and gave him a nudge with his elbow. 'But it doesn't mean I'll go easy on you in the next half.'

And for the **first time** since the game had started, Sanjay could smile.

In the change rooms, Oz was keeping his distance from everyone, pacing back and forth like he couldn't bear to stand still. But as they jogged back out onto the field, Sanjay copped it.

'I heard you speaking to **THE TRAITOR**,' Oz snapped.

Sanjay stopped, forcing Oz to stop alongside him. 'It was the **right thing to do**. I shouldn't have let him take the energy bar.'

Oz seemed to think about that for a minute. He looked like he'd swallowed something **SOUR**.

'Are we still friends?' Sanjay said, hoping against hope.

Oz looked at him in surprise. 'What? Of course we are.'

'It's just that ... you've been all about Jack this past week,' Sanjay blurted out. 'All that history you have, watching those videos and just being so ... *mad*. We've **barely spoken** all week.'

Sanjay noticed Oz glance across the oval where the Cockroaches were coming out of the change rooms. 'Yeah. I've been **a bit of a grump**, haven't I?'

Sanjay stared. 'Well, I didn't want to say anything ...'

Oz grimaced. 'Don't worry. Ellie's said **PLENTY**.'

They both watched as Jack led his team out.

'He's not a traitor, you know,' Sanjay said carefully. 'He's actually pretty cool.'

''Course he is! He was my best mate! You think I'd be friends with someone who **WASN'T** cool?' Oz's smile grew wider, until soon he was laughing.

Sanjay shook his head, and started to laugh too. 'No. I guess not.'

'Which is why you and me are **besties** now, Sanj!' Oz threw an arm around Sanjay's shoulder.

Sanjay blushed, and grinned broadly.

'Come on,' Oz said. 'We've got a game to win.'

Ellie watched Oz and Sanjay head to the huddle with their arms around each other. A knot formed in her throat.

This was meant to be fun! It was **THE BIG ONE!** All year they'd hoped this would happen – that the Falcons would play in a Grand Final, all of them together, playing their best footy, having **the time of their lives**.

Instead, Ellie was struggling to get near the ball, Sanjay had looked sick all game, and Oz was barely speaking to her.

Of course, Oz was being a **TOTAL PAIN.** And Sanjay was just encouraging him.

But still. This was **NOT** how today was meant to play out.

She'd tried everything she could to beat Jack with her height, but he was just **too tall**. And he was just too big. Jack was playing like the star he was, and Ellie had to admit it was intimidating. She tried to do what Oz said, tried to remember all the advice – mostly nagging – he'd provided.

But the truth was, it didn't **FEEL** right.

Nothing felt right.

She couldn't let the game continue with all this ... **STUFF** going on. It was time to activate **THE TWIN TAKE OFF**.

As Sanjay broke off and headed for

his position, Ellie ran towards her brother – her annoying, **super selfish** brother – and tapped him on the shoulder.

Oz turned around, his face stiff, like he was bracing for something.

'Here's the thing,' she said quickly. 'You and I need to **WORK TOGETHER** if we want to win.'

'That's what I've been *saying*!'

'But that doesn't mean I have to do everything you say. And definitely not all your way.'

'O-kay ...'

'We can win,' Ellie said. 'But it can't be all about Jack Pang.'

Oz crossed his arms. 'What is it about then?'

Ellie watched Rana warming up with a front-kick-back-kick combo. She saw Sanjay complete a two-step shuffle at the end of his **REV-UP** dance. Coach Daisy was talking to different players with Frankie on her shoulder echoing her every word, and her whole family and the rest of Fresca Bay were on the sidelines cheering and whooping in anticipation of the start of the **final quarter**.

Ellie waved vaguely at them, trying to take it all in. 'This will be why we win. **All of this.**'

Oz looked a bit puzzled, so Ellie continued.

'We're going to do **THE TWIN TAKE OFF**,' Ellie said.

Oz's face lit up and that annoying grin spread across his expression.

'But we're going to do it **MY WAY**.'

Oz's face twitched, and Ellie could see he wasn't convinced. 'That means we play to our own strengths – playing our **OWN** game. But working together.'

'Yeah. I don't know what that means,' Oz said.

She called him in closer and whispered the details of her **BRILLIANT** new plan.

Then she stepped back, watching Oz's face while her words sank in.

Oz's grin grew wider. He nodded slowly, then faster. 'I think that might work.'

'Only if we give it our best,' Ellie said.

Sanjay ran over, looking confused. 'Everything okay?'

'We're **TOTALLY FINE**,' Ellie said. 'Aren't we, Oz?'

Oz laughed. 'Yeah. I reckon we are.'

Sanjay let out a huge sigh. 'I have no idea what's going on but you both seem happy, so **let's win this thing!**'

'You better tell Sanjay the new plan,' Ellie said.

'Okay, Sanjay,' Oz began, 'You ready to break this game open?'

Sanjay's smile was as wide as the MCG.

Ellie left the boys talking, and ran to the square, taking her spot opposite Jack. **'Good luck, Jack!'**

Jack grinned and said, 'Good luck, Els!'

And right before the umpire took her spot, Ellie called out at the top of her voice. **'LET'S GO, FALCONS!'**

CHAPTER

12

Oz had played in some incredible games of footy, but this match was **NEXT LEVEL!** It had been a thriller of a Grand Final so far, like the Eagles V Pies in 2018! This was a match he'd be telling his kids about one day. And maybe their kids. And even their kids' kids!

But – it wasn't over yet. There was still **one quarter** to go.

And there was only seven points in it. Could the Falcons catch the Cockroaches?

As he waited for the final quarter to start, Oz thought about the three-quarter time huddle, and Coach Daisy's final words.

'You guys have had an **AMAZING SEASON**. No matter what happens, no-one can take that away. When you focus on fun, who cares if you've won?'

'*Focus on fun, don't fall on your bum!*' said Frankie.

Everyone had laughed.

'That is NOT what I said, Frankie!' said Daisy.

The truth was, this week hadn't been **ANYWHERE NEAR** as much fun as it should have been. And now they were about to play their **final minutes** of footy for the whole year! They had one last chance to make it right.

Jack ran past Sanjay to get to his spot in the ruck. Oz noticed him giving Sanjay a nod and a smile.

Rack off, Jack! Oz thought. *Sanjay is* **MY** *best friend!*

And then the siren sounded, and the umpire bounced the ball.

Ellie and Jack went up in the ruck. Both got a fist to the Sherrin, and it shot out sideways to Sanjay. Dancing left, then right, he **found some space**, and booted the ball long to Rana. It really clocked some distance – Tayla Harris would've been proud! Rana played on but was surrounded by Cockroach defenders.

Oz went streaming down to the forward line. 'Rana! Rana! On your right.'

She was able to tap it out to Oz, but Jumpin' Jack was giving chase. The big dude was **HOT ON HIS HEELS**.

I can beat him. I can beat him, Oz chanted to himself.

A quick soccer forward, and the Falcons were within two kicks of the goals. But instead of soccering the footy towards the goals again, Oz bent low to scoop it up.

I can beat him. **I can beat him.**

But Oz was going too fast. The thought of Jack coming from behind **SPOOKED** him, and Oz skidded over. The ball spilt out to Jack, who took off with it.

Oz scrambled to get back on his feet as Jack **SLICED** his way through the centre — one bounce, then two, twisting and turning like Lachie Neale.

NOOOO!

Oz sprinted after Jack, but the guy had

too much distance on him. He was zig-zagging around the Falcons like they were witches hats!

Jack stepped out of the square and **THUMPED** the ball long. It was a good old-fashioned torp, cutting through the air like a missile. It was a **GINORMOUS** kick!

For a moment it looked like the ball might just keep going till it hit the moon. But no, it flattened, then fell down, down, down... and through the goals for another six points to the Cockroaches!

Oz fell to his knees and **THUMPED** the ground.

For the next few minutes of play, Oz didn't take his eyes off Jack. And he didn't like what he was seeing.

Ellie's giving him too much space! She's watching the ball, not Jack. **She's gotta play in front!**

'Come on, Ellie!' cried Oz. 'Your plan's not going to work unless you can make space!'

'It's okay, Oz! I've got this!'

But time was slipping away. If they wanted to shut down Jack and win the game, Oz had to step up.

He had to do it himself.

It was an **EX-BEST FRIEND SHOWDOWN**.

Oz knew there wasn't much time left in the game. A few minutes at most? The Falcons were down by two points. But you didn't get a Premiership Cup for *almost* winning a Grand Final. They had to **DO SOMETHING** – and fast! The ball was on the wing, but it was sure to be booted back towards the centre, cos that's where Jumpin' Jack was. Oz *had* to stop him –

The ball clunked towards them, and Oz ran towards Ellie and Jack to intercept.

THUNK!

The twins COLLIDED.

'Hey!' cried Ellie as she untangled herself from her brother. 'I had him covered!'

By the time Oz wriggled free, Jack had already **BOOTED** the ball long. But fortunately for the Falcons, Freddo took a chest mark, dropping back into a hole. He handpassed to Koa, who ran around one of the shorter Cockroach players, then handpassed to Clara. Clara hoofed it right to Rana in the centre. It was building nicely.

Ellie took off. She dropped back, leading to the **far wing**. Oz spotted Jack following her, so he ran after them too.

Ellie changed directions to fool Jack, but ran **STRAIGHT TOWARDS** Oz, who wasn't looking where the ball was going. Then—

DOINK! It bopped him on the head.

Ellie and Jack both went for the ball, but it tumbled over the boundary line.

'Oz, trust me!' said Ellie, running past her

brother. 'It's time to change it up.'

'You mean **THE TWIN TAKE OFF?**' said Oz, suddenly without his usual confidence. The back of his head was **throbbing**. 'Maybe we should do it the original way?'

Ellie hesitated for one second before she shook her head. 'No. We need to **play to our strengths** – you know that. That's how a team works!' she replied.

As the ump prepared to throw the ball in, Oz had a choice: stick to Jack, or try Ellie's new version of their signature move. He glanced at Ellie. She wasn't giving Jack an inch. Jack, on the other hand, only had eyes for the ball. Had he even **noticed** Oz? What did that matter anyway?

Sanjay ran by and clapped him on the shoulder. 'You know what to do, Oz!'

And suddenly he did.

Oz ran behind Ellie. 'Let's do it!' he called as he moved past. As though she'd read his mind, Ellie jumped just at the right time, tapping the footy over her head. Oz grabbed it and booted it high. But instead of staying low himself, he let Ellie link her fingers and give him a boost instead. Just like she'd suggested.

'RRRROOOOARRRRRRRR!'

Oz roared like a lion with laryngitis as he

flew into the air in front of Jack. Ellie had launched him perfectly into the sky, and he kinda enjoyed being the decoy. It was also fun seeing Jack's face. The guy was clearly **SHOCKED** by the take off!

At the same time, Sanjay positioned himself for the mark. He took it cleanly as Ellie cheered him on. Oz saw Jack glance at Sanjay, wondering what happened. Oz gave another roar for good measure. The siren was sure to sound any second!

This kick could win the Grand Final.

Sanjay booted the ball **HARD**. It was a wobbly old kick but it had some **OOMPH**.

Oz gritted his teeth. The footy angled

up in the air. It bent this way and that—

Hoooooooonk!

The siren sounded ... Oz counted five **AGONISING** seconds before—

WHOOSH!

The footy passed through the big sticks!

A goal! A win!

THE FALCONS WERE THE PREMIERS!

The whole crowd **ERUPTED!** Spectators ran onto the oval, and the Falcons players all rushed to the goal square where Sanjay was celebrating his Premiership-winning kick.

Oz ran over to his cousin, but instead of

high fives and bear hugs, Oz went straight into Sanjay's **VICTORY DANCE!**

'You were listening!' Sanjay's face lit up and he joined Oz.

As the two boys danced their routine, Ellie joined them, then Rana and all the other Falcons. Within minutes, all the Littles, Coach Daisy, Mrs Tan, Ms Miffy-Osborne and even Principal Wylie got in on the act, with Ginger's mums leading the way! It was like a **flash mob** in the goal square.

Hips left, hips right, twist and jump before their big finish – a super loud **'EEEEEEEEEEEEP!'**

CHAPTER

13

An hour later, Sanjay's body was covered in energy drink. That was apparently how you celebrated a Grand Final win. He was super sticky, but still super pumped. The Falcons had been partying for over an hour in the change rooms. But Sanjay wanted to step outside to take a breather (and maybe **dry off** in the sun, too).

The Cockroaches were leaving their change rooms as well. A few had their heads down looking a bit glum, but most were chatting. One even mentioned coming back **'bigger and better next year'**.

We'll see about that! thought Sanjay.

Jack was last to leave, but he stopped to do up his shoelaces. Then he spotted Sanjay, and gave him a small smile. Sanjay wiped the energy drink off his face.

'GOOD GAME, JACK.'

'Thanks Sanj,' said Jack. 'Just wasn't our year.'

Sanjay noticed Oz hovering in the

doorway. He waved his cousin over.

Oz hesitated, but then joined Jack and Sanjay, a crooked smile on his face.

'We should all grab a **milkshake** at Manny's sometime,' Sanjay said, feeling braver now.

Before either could answer, Ellie poked her head through the doorway. 'Or do you wanna come over for pizzas, Jack?'

'Aww, thanks guys, but I'm not really up for celebrating right now,' said Jack.

'Not tonight,' said Ellie. '*Tomorrow*. Dad wants to celebrate the **Maths Championship** win. He's cooking up a feast!'

'Oh. Right.' Jack glanced uncertainly at Oz.

'When Dad cooks, he cooks **A LOT**,' Oz said, grinning broadly. 'I **probably** won't be able to eat it all.'

Jack's grin matched Oz's. 'Is that right?'

'You might as well help out,' Oz added.

Jack's smile grew. 'That'd be cool.' He waved at Ellie and Sanjay. 'Thanks! See you then.'

After Jack left, Sanjay, Oz and Ellie stood on the sidelines, staring in awe at the oval where they'd just won the **BIG ONE**, each one of them wearing a **HUGE** cheesy grin.

'We did it!' said Ellie.

'Yup!' said Oz. 'Nice work, you guys. The **TWIN TAKE OFF** for the win!'

Ellie groaned. 'We **REALLY** need to stop calling it that. Especially now you're part of the thing, hey Sanjay?'

Sanjay shrugged, but his belly felt warm and he could have sworn his face was **glowing**. 'I mean, that is a pretty cool name.'

'Yeah, but it's not a **TWIN THING**, is it?' Oz said.

'Nope,' said Ellie. 'It's a Little thing.'

Oz scrunched up his face, seeming to think hard. Then his eyes lit up and he said, 'I've got it! Let's call it, **THE LITTLE LIFT OFF!**'

Ellie laughed. 'That sounds right.'

The warmth in Sanjay's belly seemed to swell. He couldn't stop grinning as Oz gave Sanjay a high five.

'So, Sanj,' Ellie said. 'What did you think of your first season of **AUSSIE RULES?**'

Sanjay thought hard for a minute, not sure he could find the words. He stood suddenly straighter, shifted his feet into second position, then leapt high in a jetè, before breaking into a whole new dance routine that mixed the **rev-up dance** with the celebration dance, with some hip-hop thrown in.

Ellie and Oz **CHEERED** as he went through his steps.

Just as he finished, Oz sang the first notes of the Falcons theme song, and, as though answering the call, Rana, Ginger, Koa, Freddo, Chiara, Clara, Olivia and all the Falcons burst out of the club rooms and joined in. And soon they were all singing at the top of their lungs, all the little legends **perfectly in tune**.

MEET THE TEAM!

Fresca Bay
FALCONS

BOOKS
9

AWARDS
3

#1
FOOD
gingerbread

#1
COLOUR
purple

AUTHOR

NICOLE HAYES

200

AFL

NICOLE HAYES

is an award-winning author, a podcaster with The Outer Sanctum and a footy fanatic. She's a **HUGE** Hawks fan.

ADRIAN BECK

is a part-time TV
producer, part-time
writer and full-time
AFL fan. He barracks
for St Kilda.

Want to find out what else the FRESCA BAY FALCONS have been getting up to?

BOOK 1

OZZY RULES!

AFL Little LEGENDS

OZZY RULES!

JAMES HART

NICOLE HAYES & ADRIAN BECK

Oz and Ellie Little are **FOOTY FANATICS**. They can't wait to introduce Aussie Rules to their cousin Sanjay, a **footy newbie!**

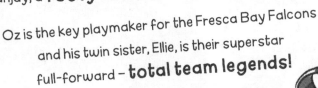

Oz is the key playmaker for the Fresca Bay Falcons and his twin sister, Ellie, is their superstar full-forward – **total team legends!**

But when Sanjay tries footy for the first time, he's a **NATURAL**. Suddenly, Sanjay is the Falcons' hot new recruit and Oz has some **serious** competition.

Can Oz handle sharing the spotlight, or will his competitive spirit cause tension for the team?

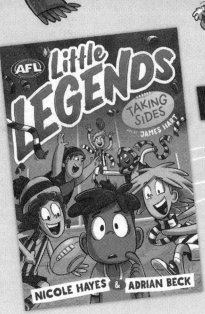

BOOK 2

TAKING SIDES

Sanjay is settling in **PERFECTLY** at **Fresca Bay**.

He loves hanging out with his cousins Oz and

Ellie, and playing footy for the Fresca Bay

Falcons is heaps of fun.

But when he wins a prize to meet the **AFL TEAM**

of his choice, things suddenly get

a lot more complicated.

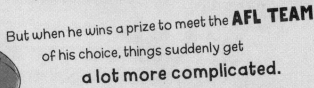

SANJAY HASN'T PICKED A TEAM YET!

All at once, everyone Sanjay knows is giving him their opinion

on which team to follow – but **WHO** will Sanjay choose?

And will he crack under pressure?

BOOK 3

GO FOR GOAL!

AFL Little LEGENDS

GO FOR GOAL!
by JAMES HART

NICOLE HAYES & ADRIAN BECK

ELLIE IS IN A GOAL-KICKING SLUMP.

She has a feeling her brand-new footy boots are to blame – that, or her brother Oz and all the annoying pranks he keeps playing on her!

Is it possible that without her old pair of lucky boots, Ellie just isn't that good at footy?

Or is footy about **MORE** than just **LUCK**?